Chaucer's First Winter

For Peter, who has always liked winter.
—S. K.

Acknowledgments

With many thanks to Laurent and Navah,
for all your help and good humor.
—H. C.

SIMON & SCHUSTER BOOKS FOR YOUNG READERS
An imprint of Simon & Schuster Children's Publishing Division
1230 Avenue of the Americas, New York, New York 10020
Text copyright © 2008 by Stephen Krensky
Illustrations copyright © 2008 by Henry Cole
The illustrated depiction of the Ty Inc. plush toy bear is used with the permission of Ty Inc. © 2008, Ty Inc.
All rights reserved. TY, the Ty Heart Logo, and TY CLASSIC are all trademarks owned by Ty Inc.
All rights reserved, including the right of reproduction in whole or in part in any form.
SIMON & SCHUSTER BOOKS FOR YOUNG READERS is a trademark of Simon & Schuster, Inc.
Book design by Laurent Linn
The text for this book is set in Alghera.
The illustrations for this book are rendered in acrylic paint, colored pencil, and ink on Arches hot press watercolor paper.
Manufactured in China
2 4 6 8 10 9 7 5 3
The Library of Congress has cataloged a prior printing as follows:
Krensky, Stephen.
Chaucer's first winter / Stephen Krensky ; illustrated by Henry Cole.
— 1st ed.
p.   cm.
Summary: A curious young bear, who does not want to miss the delights of winter,
skips his first hibernation to play in the snow, glide on the ice,
and admire the glittering rows of icicles and snow-covered pine trees.
ISBN-13: 978-1-4169-7479-6 (hardcover)
ISBN-10: 1-4169-7479-2 (hardcover)
[1. Bears—Fiction. 2. Hibernation—Fiction. 3. Winter—Fiction.]
I. Cole, Henry, ill. II. Title.
PZ7.K883Cf 2008   [E]—dc22   2008011224

ISBN: 978-1-4169-9026-0

Chaucer's First Winter

STEPHEN KRENSKY · ILLUSTRATED BY HENRY COLE

Simon & Schuster Books for Young Readers

New York   London   Toronto   Sydney

Chaucer was a curious, young bear.
He poked and prodded wherever he pleased—
    under rocks, under water, even high in the trees.

Chaucer's best friends were Nugget and Kit.
They were a little older than he was.

"This winter," said Nugget,
     "we're going to miss you a lot."
"Really?" asked Chaucer.
     "Where will I be while you're missing me?"
"Sleeping," said Kit. "That's just what bears do."

Chaucer's parents admitted that this news was true.

"Bears do like to snooze," his father observed.

"It's very restful," his mother added,

"which is good for growing bears."

Chaucer was not convinced.

Pretty soon, it was time for the bears' winter nap.
Chaucer's parents closed their eyes and began
softly snoring.
Chaucer was still wide awake.

So he stood up. He stretched.
Then he went back outside.

White flakes were tumbling through the air.

Chaucer caught one on his nose and two on his tongue.

They were wet to the touch and then melted away.

"It's magic," he said.

His friends were very surprised to see him.
"Why aren't you sleeping?" asked Nugget.

"I was curious," said Chaucer. "I wanted to see what winter was all about."

Kit nodded. "Well, first we must teach you what to know about snow."

Chaucer was ready.

Chaucer saw that snow made everything look different.

"It's like the land is wearing a disguise," he thought.

He paused uncertainly at the top of one familiar hill.

"How do we get to the bottom?" he asked.

"You'll *see*," said Kit.

And they had themselves a wild ride.

Over the next few days Chaucer
learned all about snowball fights.

After a month, the pond froze over.
"Careful," said Nugget, as they stepped out.
Kit nodded. "You have to get used to it."

Chaucer's paws felt funny on the ice.

He was much better at sliding than gliding.

Chaucer loved everything about winter—
the glittering rows of icicles, the pine trees dressed in white.

He even enjoyed the coldest winter nights.

One gray morning, Chaucer, Nugget,
   and Kit were out exploring.
It started to snow. And it started to blow.
Chaucer sniffed the air deeply and began
   making giant snowballs.
"This is not a good time to play," said Kit.

But Chaucer knew what he was doing.

Chaucer headed back to his family's cave.
When he got there, his parents seemed to be
just waking up.

The storms grew gentler after that.
The sun got stronger and the days
seemed longer.
"There's a change coming," said Nugget.
Kit took a deep breath. "I can almost
smell the flowers."

But Chaucer was sorry to see winter go.

He built them a safe place to watch the storm pass.

"Wait till you hear about winter!"
    said Chaucer. "There's so much to do."
"Really?" asked his mother.
"Who would have guessed?" his father added.
Chaucer wanted to tell them all about snow
    and ice and sledding down hills.
He really did.

But the rest of his story was going to have to wait.